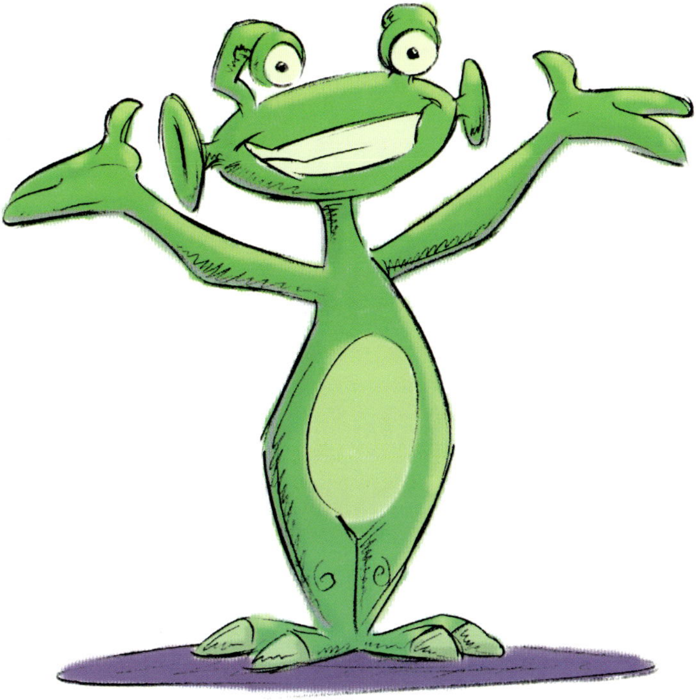

Illustrated by Raymond McGrath

Rigby

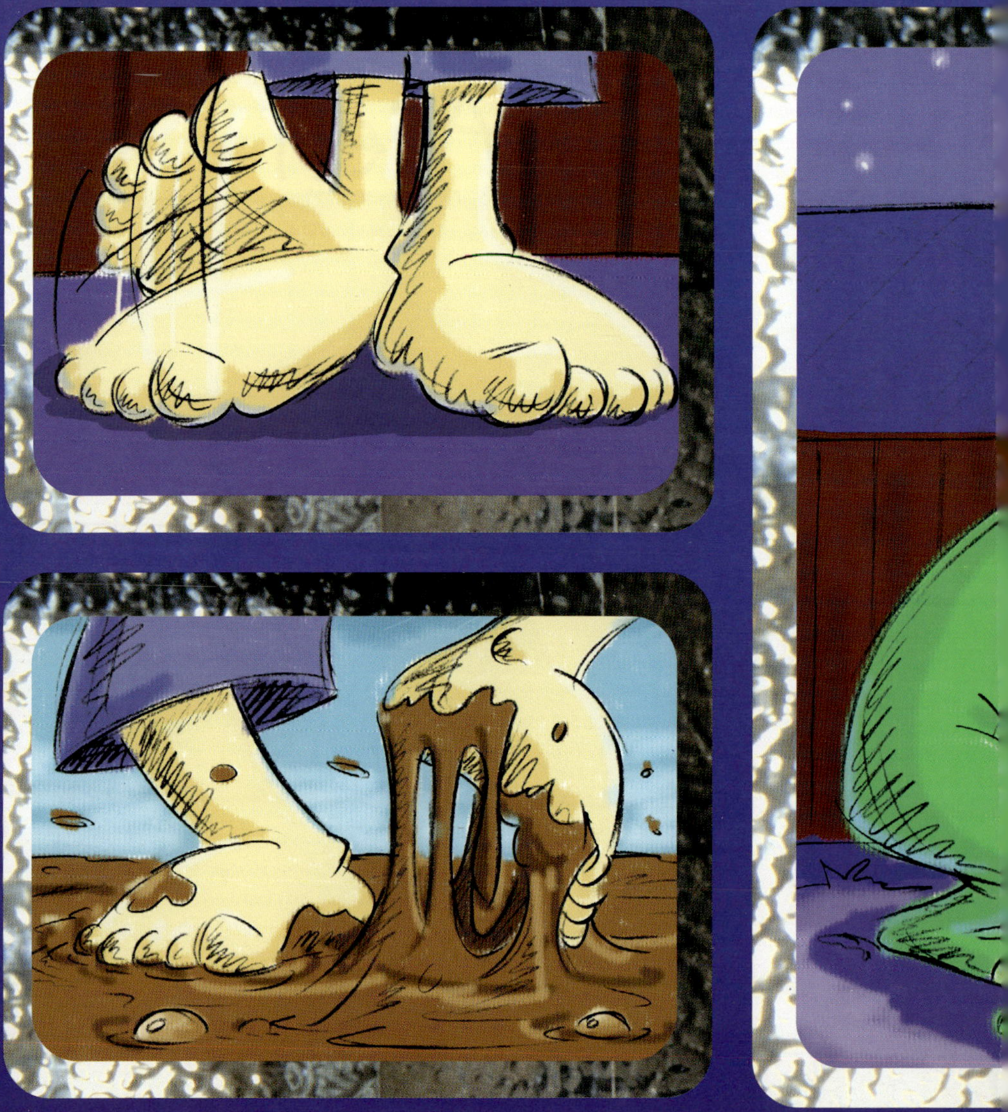

my feet

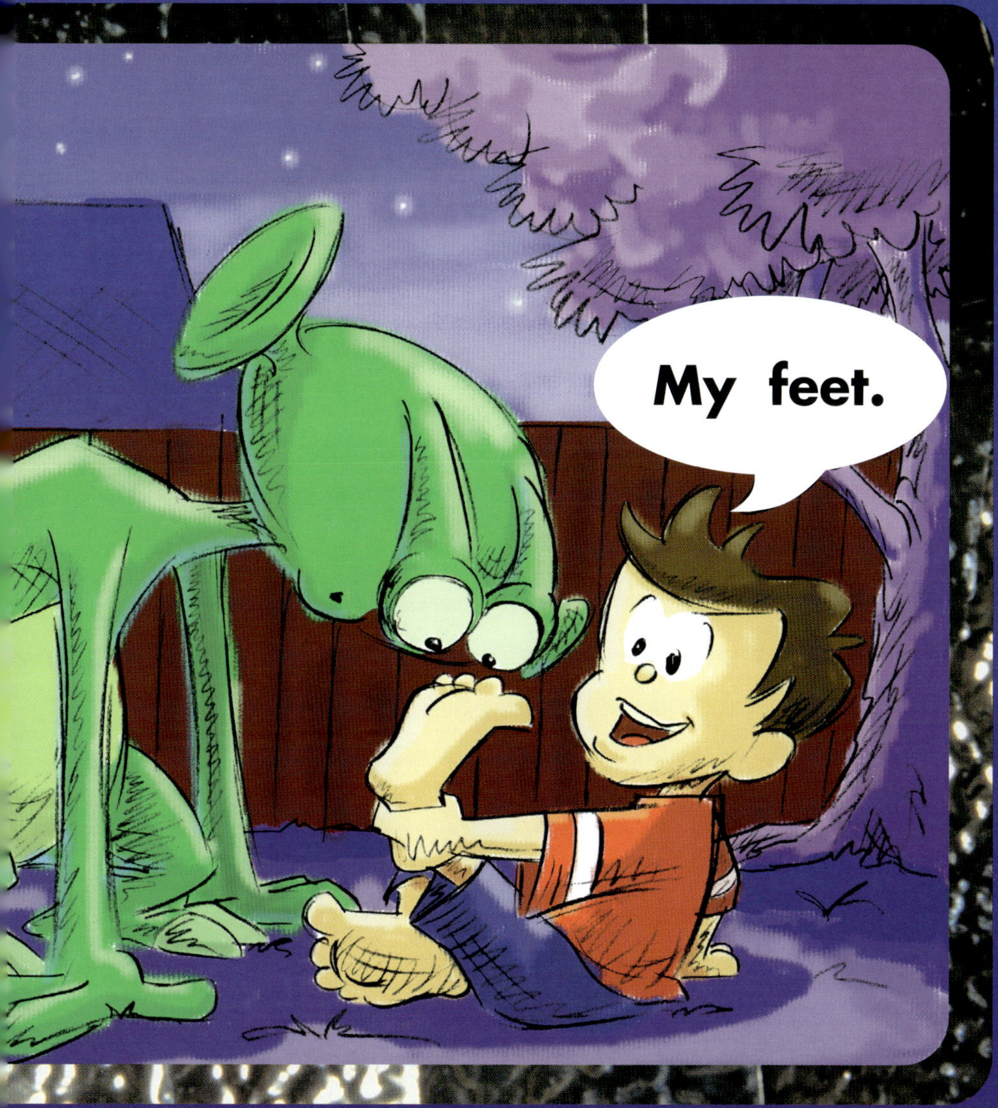
My feet.

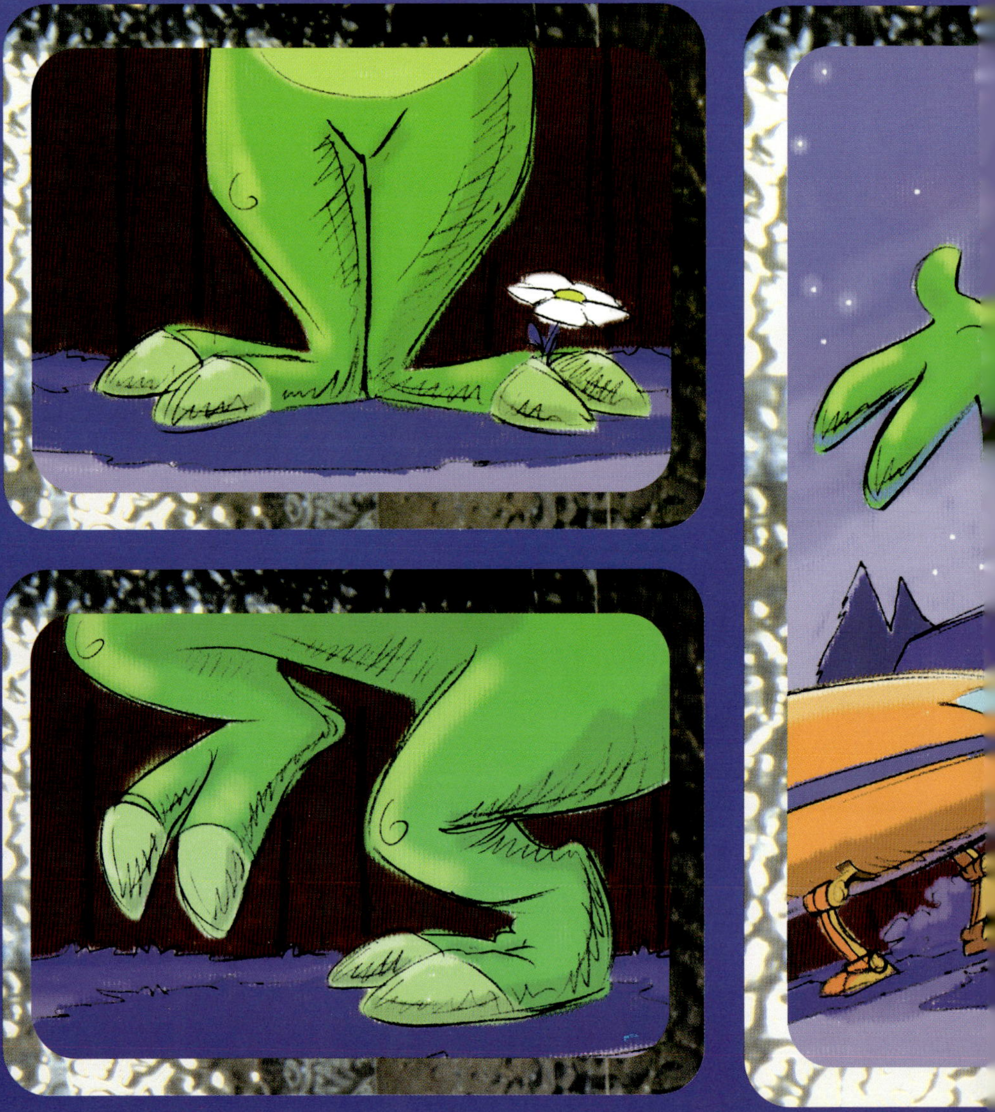

my feet

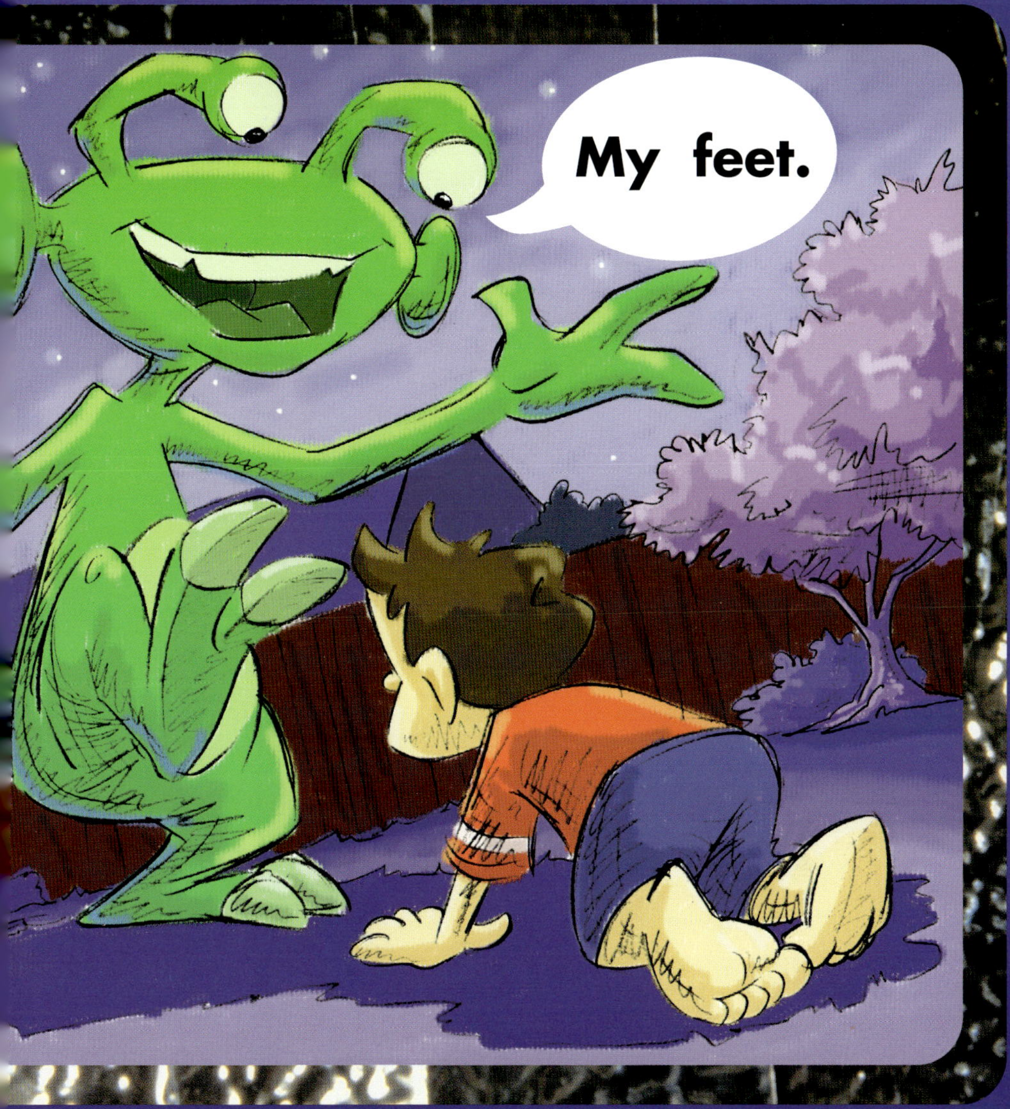
My feet.

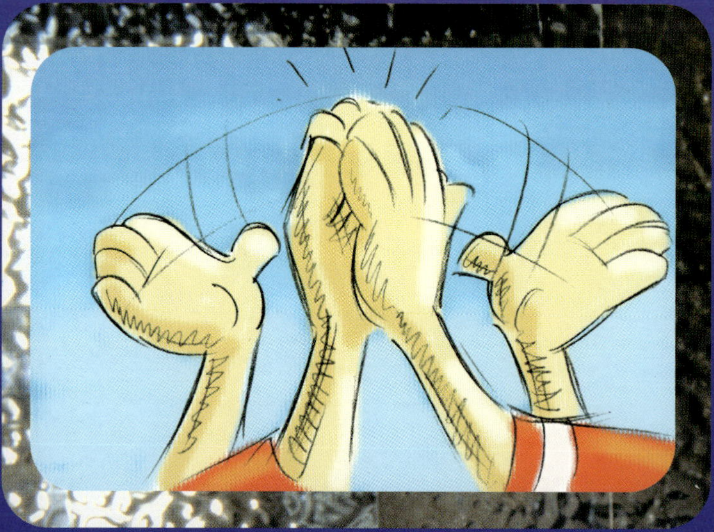

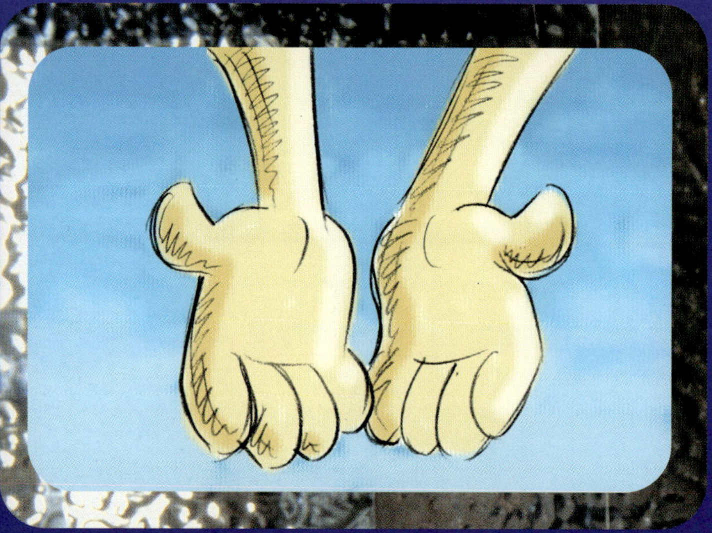

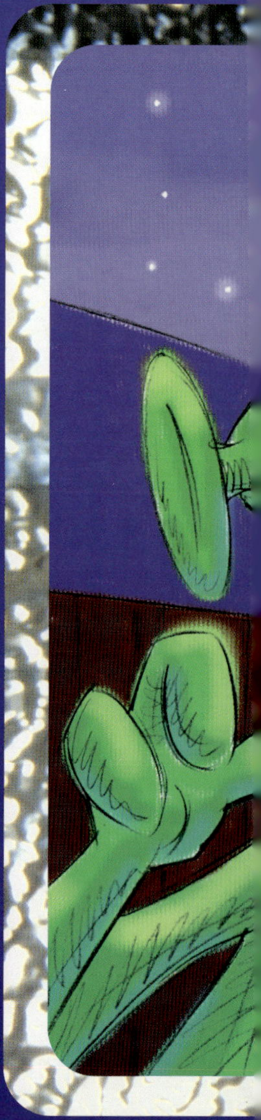

my hands

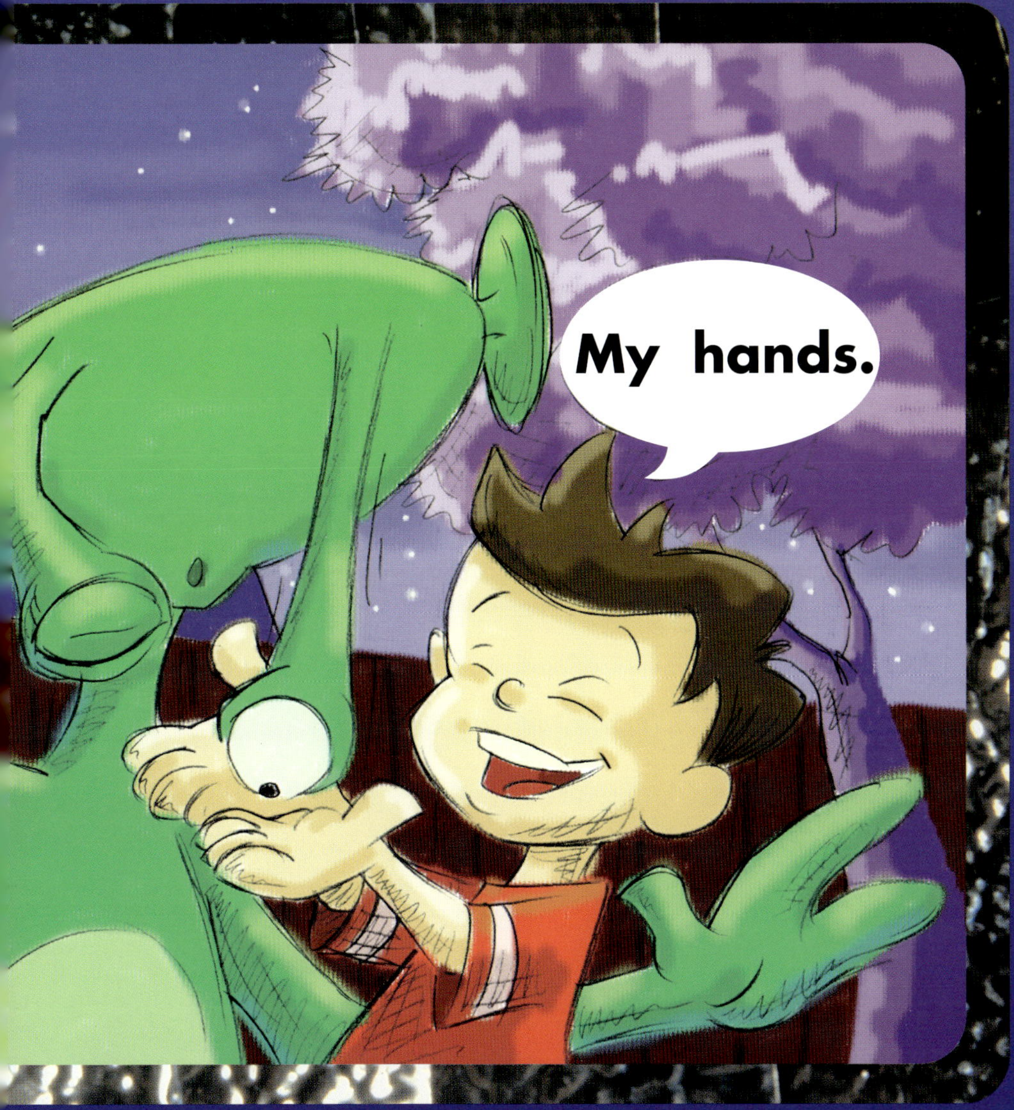
My hands.

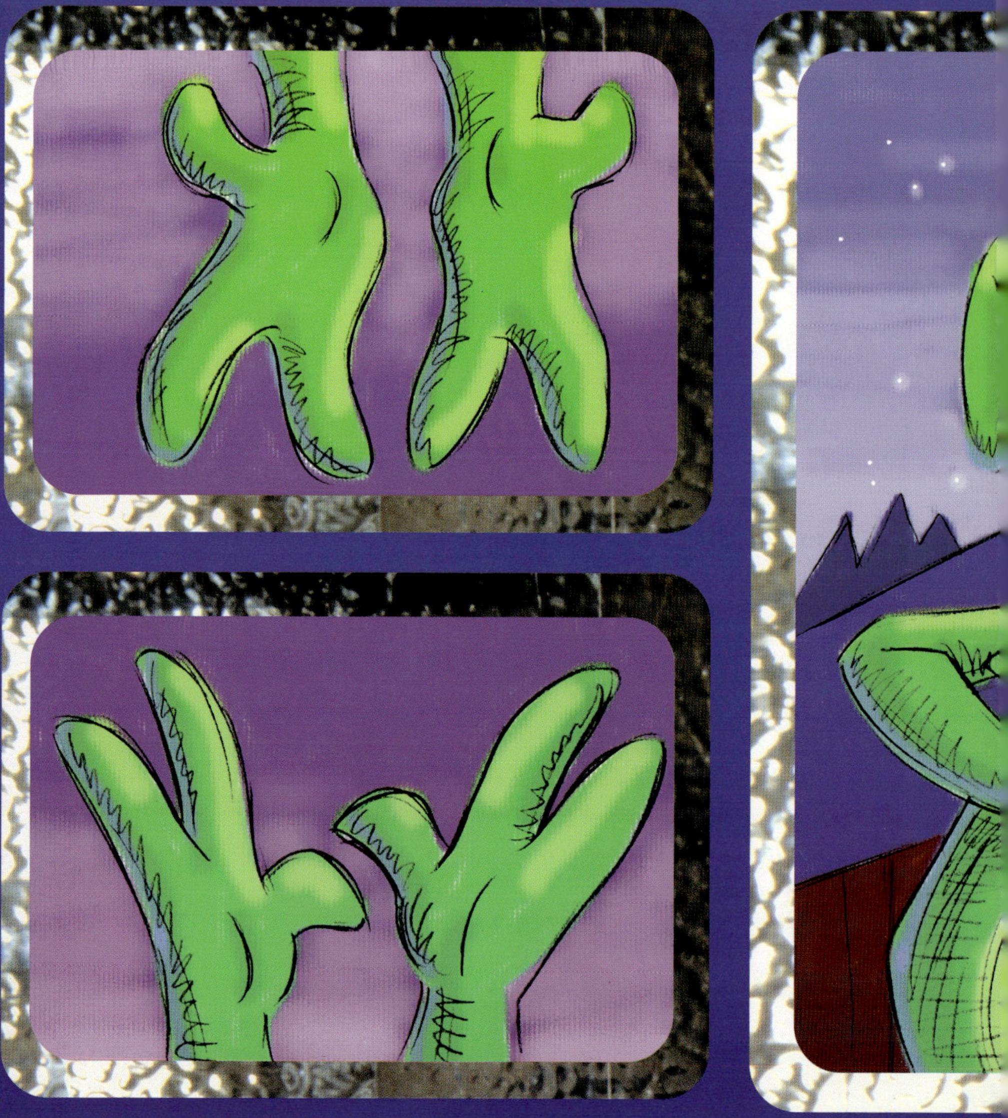

my hands

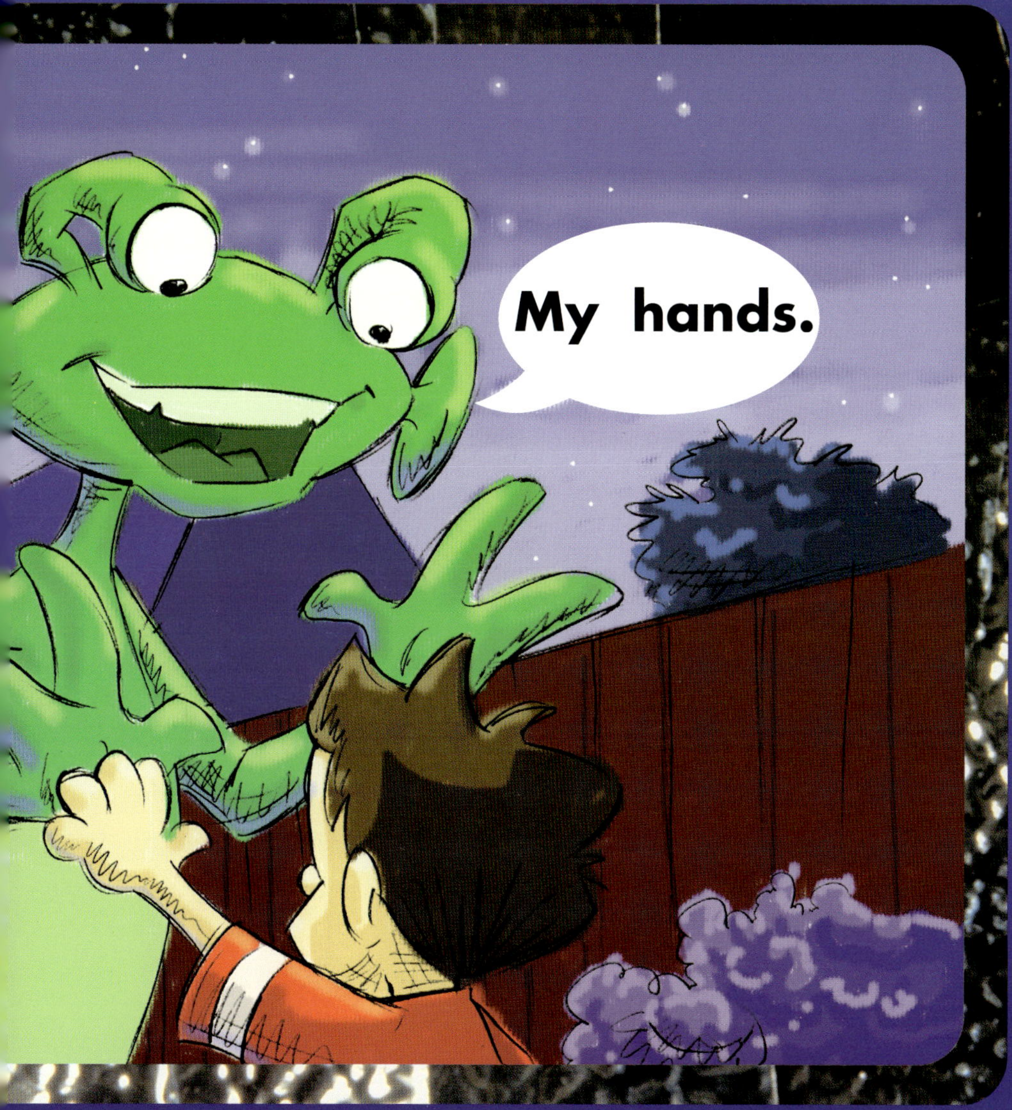
My hands.

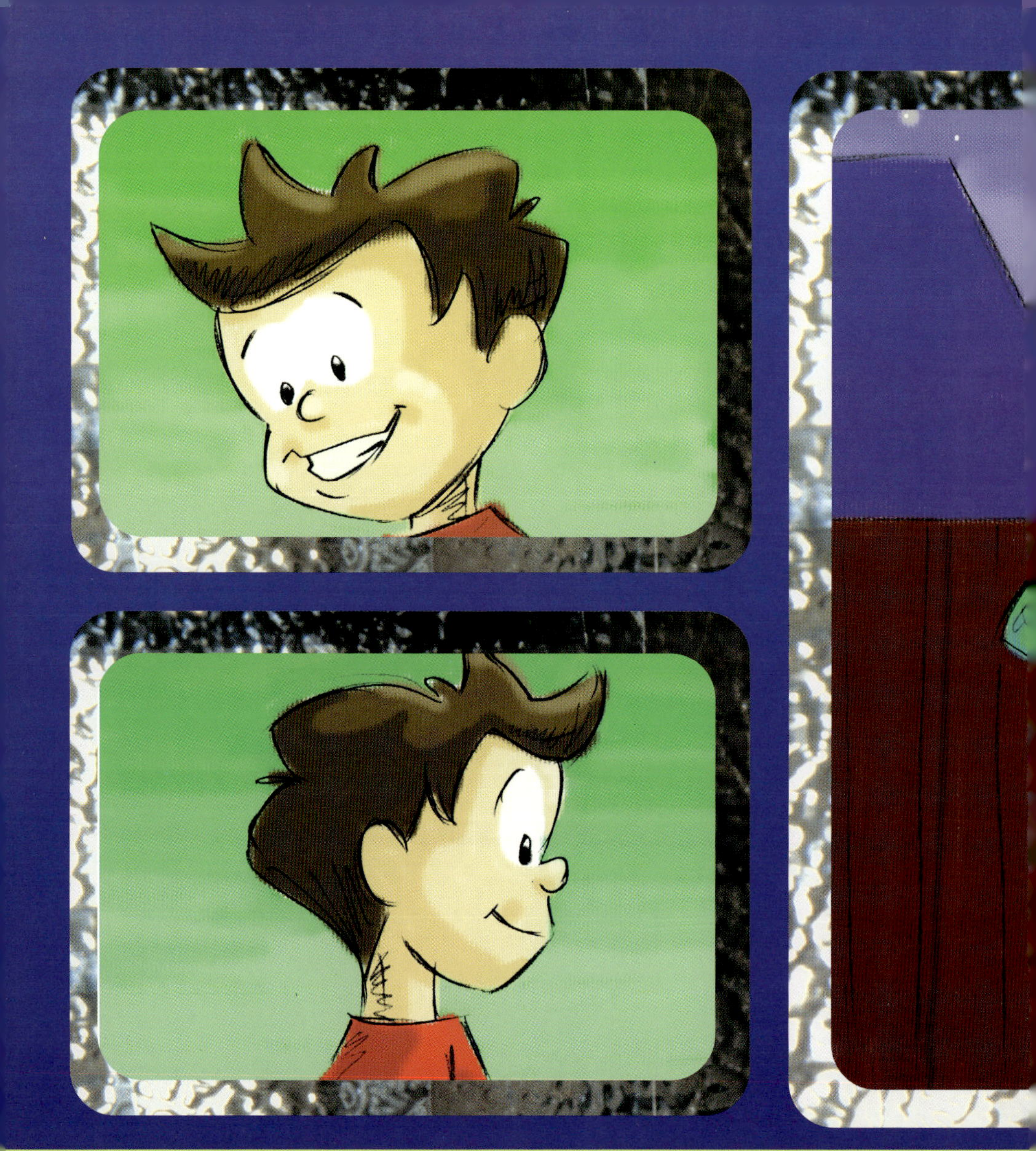

my head

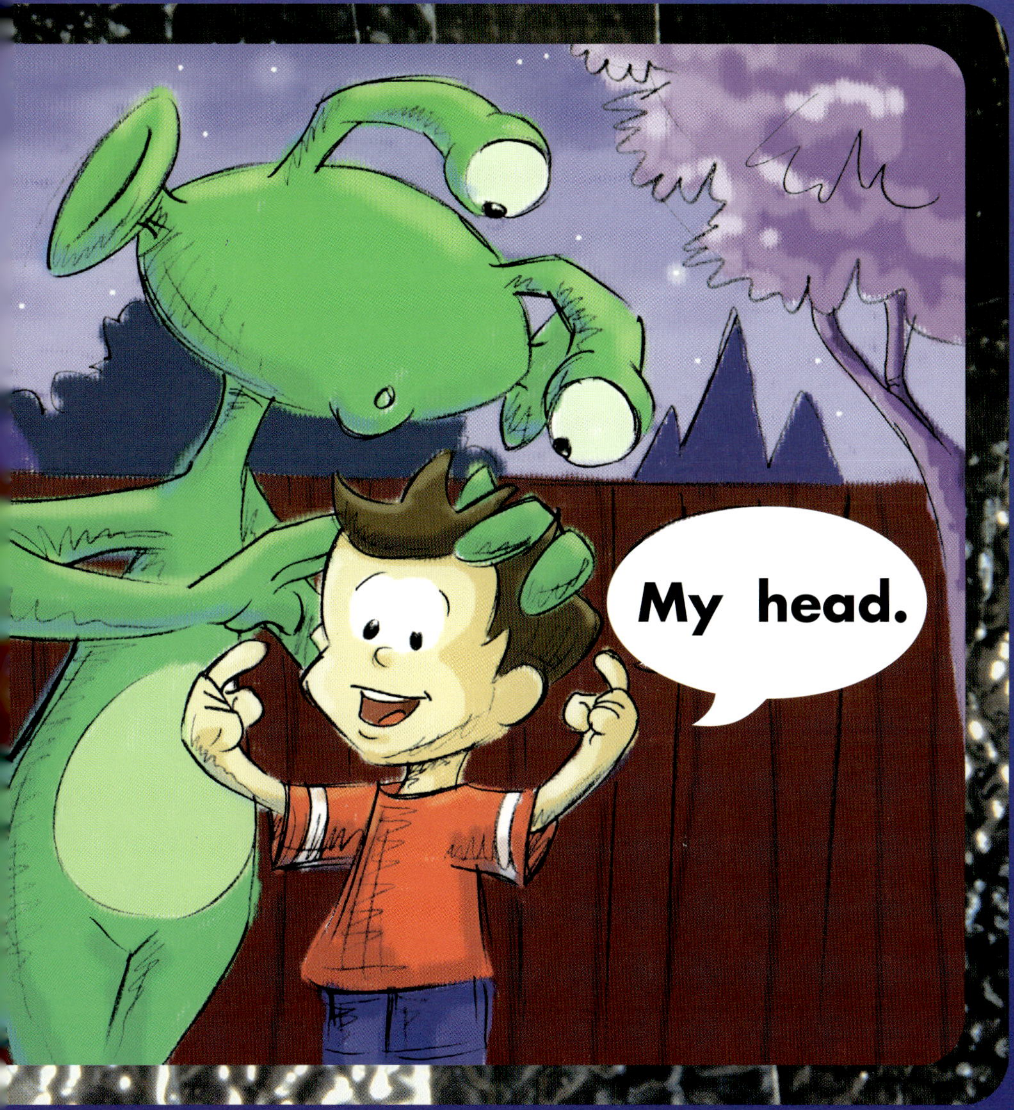
My head.

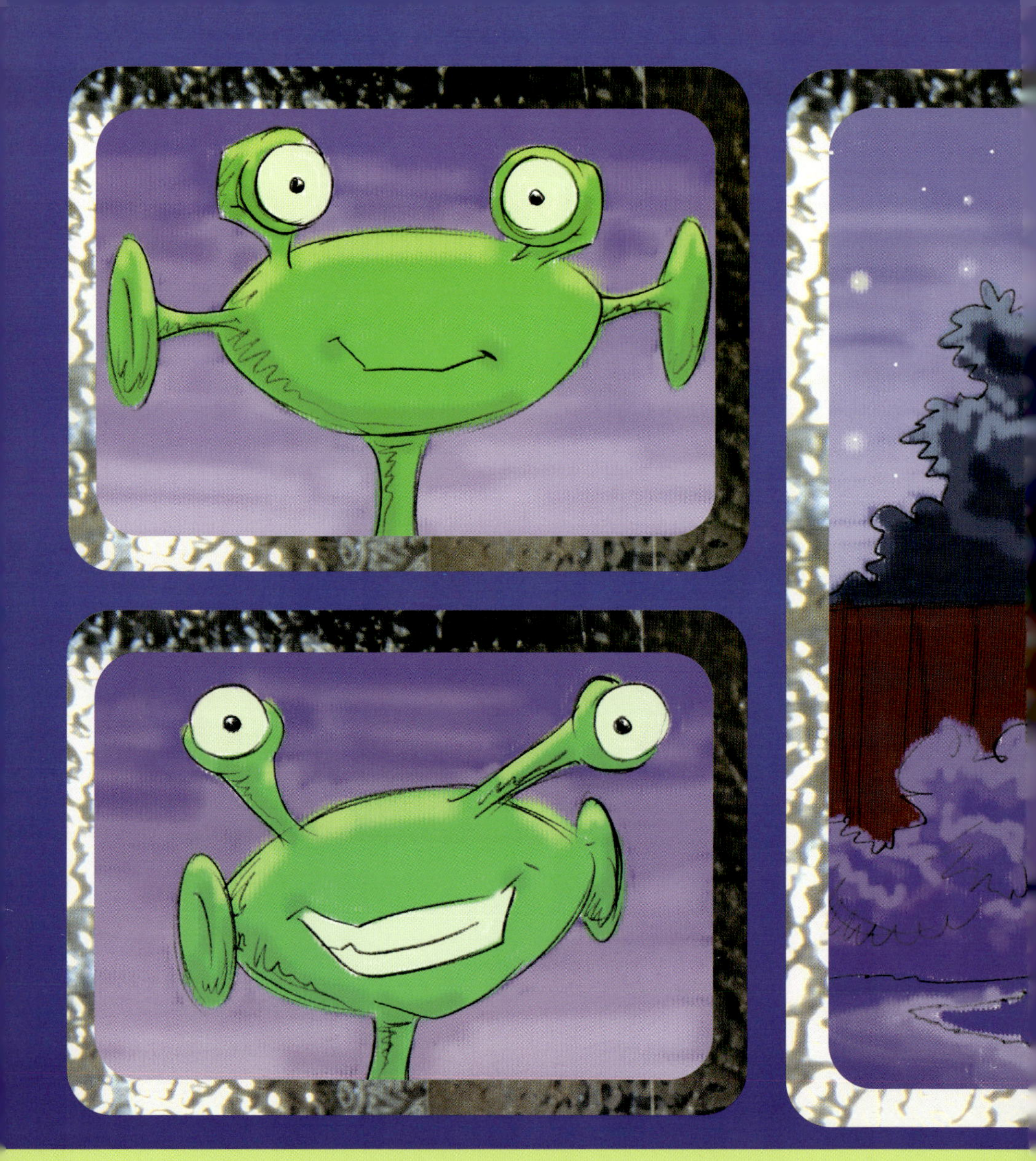

my head

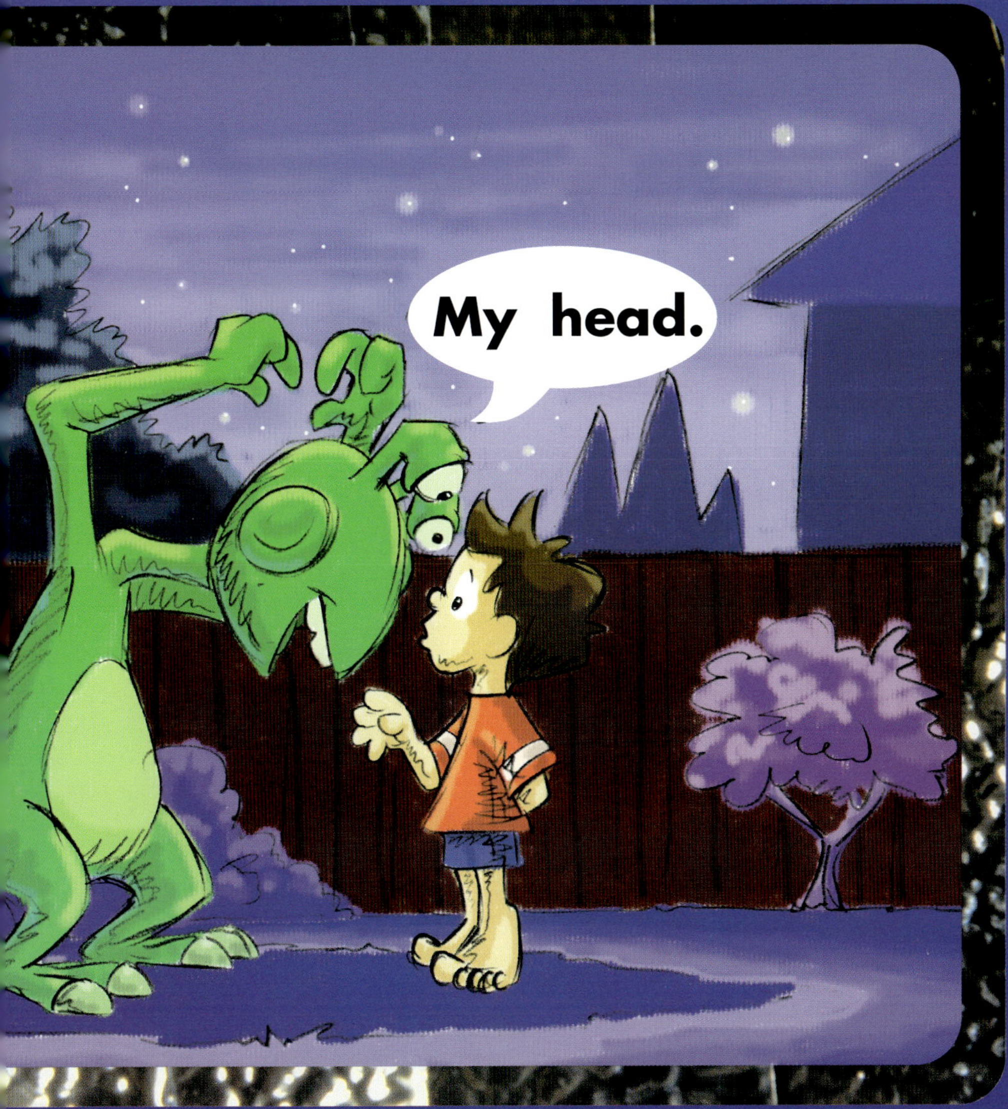
My head.

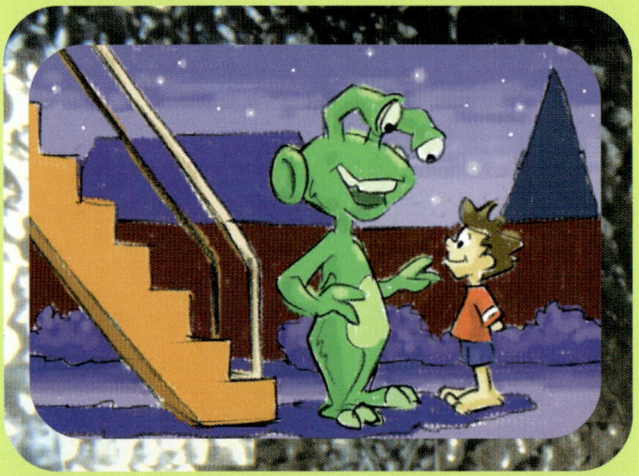

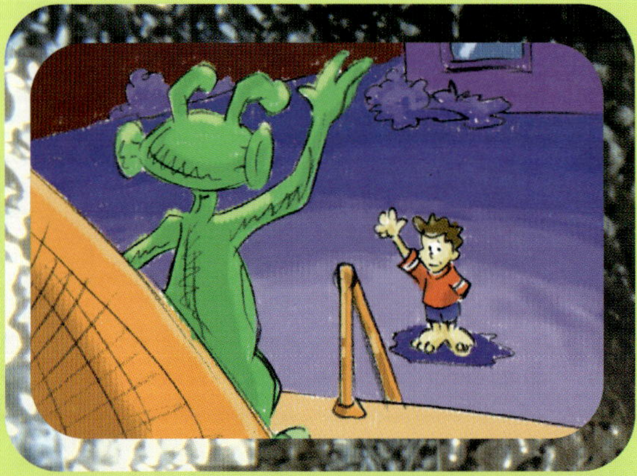

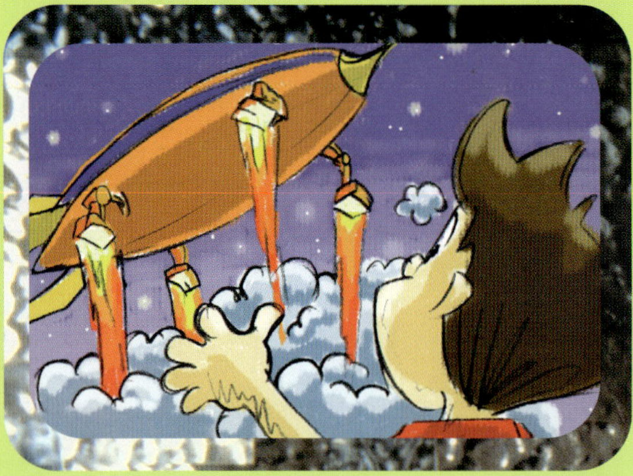

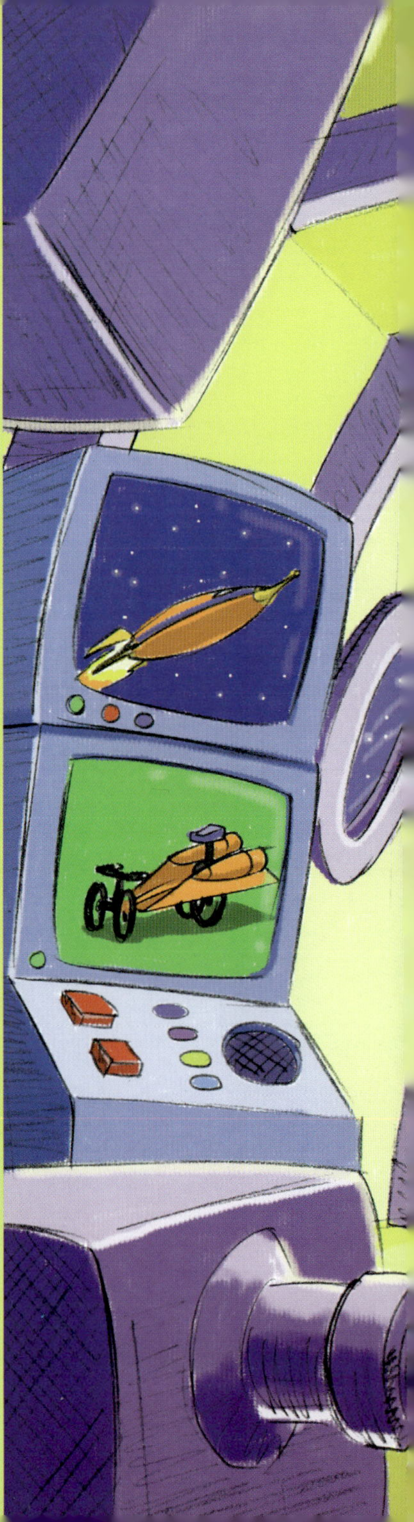

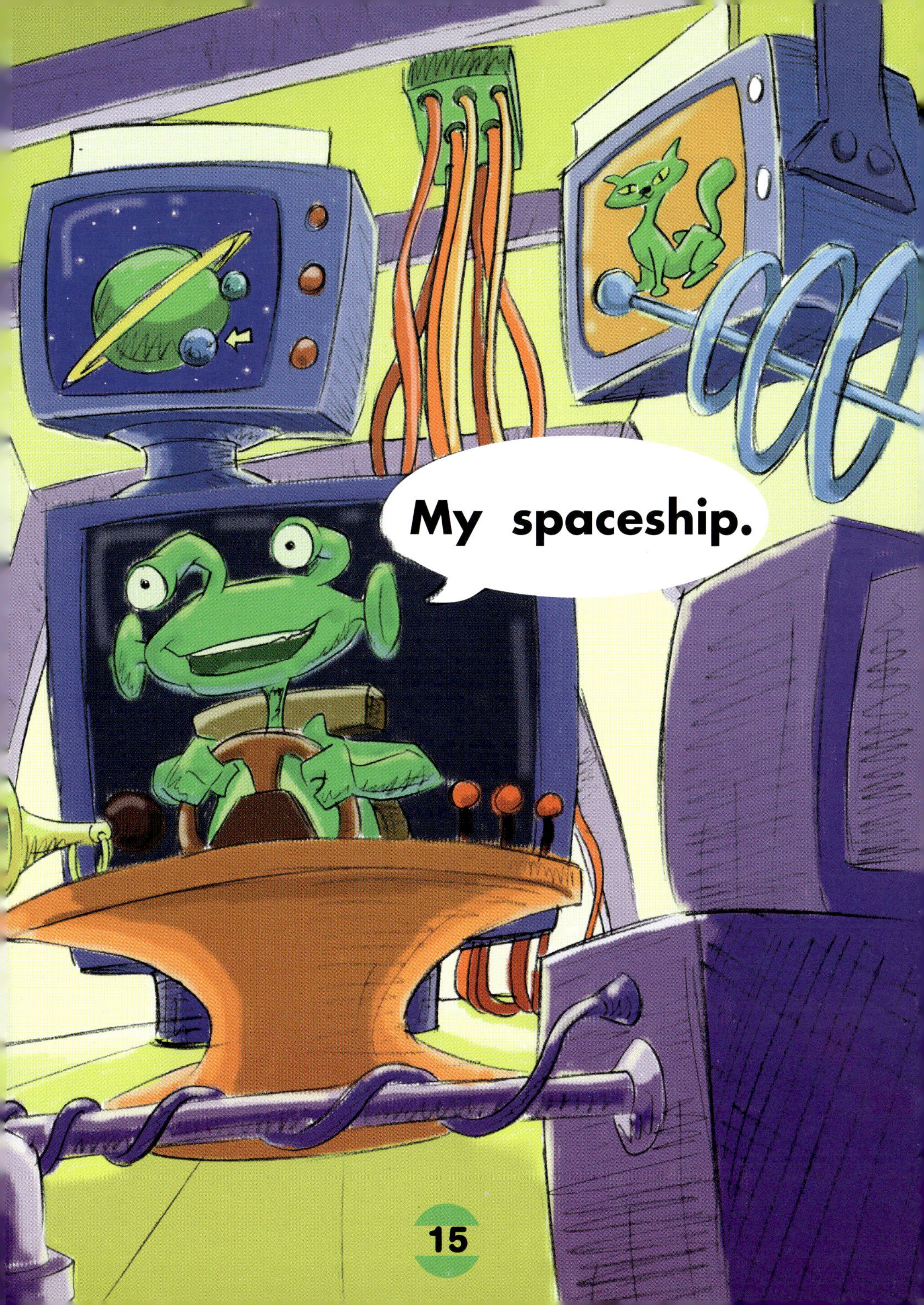
My spaceship.

is

my

me

the

my

is